ENIGMATIC LOVER

THE INCEPTION OF MYSTERY

MEENAKSHI. PILLAI

To you, yes. My sincerest gratitude and immense confidence regarding becoming an author go out to the person holding and looking at this book.

Contents

PREFACE

An innocent girl strives to get deattch from a magical, enigmatic person she fell in love with.

Acknowledgements

Finally, I'd I additionally thank my bestfriend Kapil sagar for being with me and supporting me to pop out with this book, I am feeling so blessed and would really like to comprehend my parents to encourage and to aid me to this extend.

Prologue

On the internet, she gradually builds a strong relationship with Kapil Sharma and falls in love with him. They both ended up in the middle of a terrible mystery. She ultimately forms a strong attachment to him, which has disastrous implications for her.

I

The Hypnotic Voice

In her first year of Bcom, Kalpana Iyer realized how lonely she was when her only friend, Pooja, decided to study fashion design in Chennai while she stayed in the small town of Tamil Nadu.Neither of them would have the courage to leave what they had in common.

7Having lost her father in an unexpected accident at age 15, Kalpana was so traumatized that her mother, Kalyani, moved to this small town, Hosur, and worked as a single parent to take care of her.

Despite the fact that Pooja knew Kalpana was lonely due to her, Kalpana inclined to sign up for an online dating site; she isn't as bold as Pooja, but she always wanted a love marriage so she followed her friend's advice.

Earlier that night, she downloaded an application called "LET'S Talk" from the playstore, but after exploring it, she found it useless and uninstalled it immediately.

Pooja called Kalpana the next morning and asked,

"Have you tried the app Let's Talk?" She asked. "How is it?

" *Kalpana replied with a harsh tone,"It's trash. Everyone there is eager to have sex conversations. So I uninstalled it."*"

The app's dark side was well-known to Pooja, so she responded,

""See Kalpana, it is challenging to find a best friend like me or a good partner in an random application , I know you miss me i will try to be there often still then learn to make new friends.""

Shekar's parents opposed their marriage, so Kalyani and Shekar eloped and got married. When Kalyani lost her husband in an unmerciful accident, nobody felt sympathy for Kalyani. At that time, most people assumed Kalyani would find another husband for herself. But Kalyani was a devoted wife and mother to her only daughter, Kalpana. Which is why Kalpana is very conscious about never hurting her mother, as she loves her very much.

That night, Kalpana found a website that has a singing app named "Singer Maker." Here, many people talk to each other by creating rooms and groups. It was not a typical dating app, but a good singing platform to meet and explore talented people all around the world. Kalpana was comfortable going with the app as she loved singing and found it would be a good place to continue her singing hobby as well.

Two days passed. She went through many rooms and queed and sang songs. People found her voice very mesmerising and loved getting connected with her. Among them was Kapil Sharma. Kalpana was mesmerised by the way he spoke the first time she heard him in the pary room, and the tone of his deep, hypnotic voice made her feel familiar with him.That was the first time Kalpana texted someone in Singer Maker's Inbox.

II

The blossoming of
love.

Kapil reminded Kalpana of someone she knew. She liked his polished and courteous manner of communicating, so she immediately texted him in her inbox.

"Kalpana: Hello, I was with you. You have a captivating voice, and I enjoyed the song "Chandi Jaisa Rang" that you performed.

Kapil: Thank you very much. Is this your picture for your profile? Your eyes are just stunning."

Kalpana's eyes are large and expressive. She had a less-than fair skin tone, but her hair and eyes grew so exquisite that humans used to lavish praise on her.

""Where are you from?" Kalpana texted. Are you an Indian from the south?

"No, I'm from Moradabad, North India," Kapil responded."

Kapil grew into a tall, wide, and attractive man, 7 years Kalpana's senior. who is more open-minded than Kalpana and enjoys conversing with new people.

Kalpana hesitated to keep in touch with him since she had spent some time in Delhi at the time and had heard many stories of girls being abused and sex assaulted. She was narrow-minded and assumed Kapil to be the same.

However, when Kalpana became closer to him that night, she noticed how sweet and gently he spoke to her. He hadn't made her feel uneasy in a long time, so they both went forward and dialled their number.

Kapil was well-versed in astrology, ankshatra, and other related subjects.

During the late-night call, Kapil imparted to her all the beginnings of a complicated Astro mystery and its meaning, as he had a comprehensive knowledge of astrology and ankshatra.

"Kapil, you are incredible.

The way you interpret my stars and sun signs excites me. In addition, you are correct; I am a struggler. I've struggled a lot since I was born as taurine under the Rohini star. Sagittarius, in my experience, is fortunate, but they typically manage to meet it. I'd like to find out how I can make my wish come true.

Kalpana, you are true. Yes, if you want your wishes to come true, always request them at 11:11. It's a miracle time in the cosmos, and I've double-checked that all of your wishes are fulfilled at this time."

Kapil and Kalpana's fascinating verbal discussions about myths and astros lasted all night, and they unexpectedly slept through the call.

Kalpana was late for class the next day, and she spent the rest of her time at university in a rush. She grew content and absorbed in him, and she was ready to return home and tell Kapil about her university experiences. When she got home in the evening, she dialled Pooja's number.

"Good day, Pooja. I met this guy in the Singer Maker app, and he's genuinely nice and attractive.

Great job, Kalpana, but try to recognise him as much as possible and speak about yourself as little as possible.

Okay, pooj. I'm guessing he's trying to reach me. I'll give you a call later."

Both were on call that night once again. As love is an ocean, and every devoted follower usually goes with the tide, Kalpana was engrossed in him. They continued to contact themselves often.

III

Outbreak Of Virus

They planned to meet after three years. As he awaited the completion of her bachelor's degree, Kapil planned to propose to her face-to-face. So, after a year of waiting, they began to plan their visit. The outbreak of corona engulfed the whole news channel that evening in December 2019. People were affected in such an unanticipated way, and the spread was seen in many nations within a few weeks.

Meanwhile, Kapil dailled Kaplana when he heard this.

"Kalpana, We'll meet up soon. I'm hoping that this infection will be eradicated shortly."

They both assumed the issue could be controlled, but it wasn't the same. Months passed, yet the news and the transmission of the virus continued. In the meanwhile, India has proclaimed a state of emergency. This irritated Kapil immensely. He was absolutely broken, but Kalpana was able to calm him. Month after months went by, and Things were rapidly deteriorating. Kapil was dying to actually meet Kalpana.

Kalpana didn't get a call from Kapil all of a sudden, and she assumed he was upset, but that he would contact her soon. Pooja was in Chennai as well, and she dailled Kalpana.

"Greetings, Kalpana What's happening with you? Is everything okay for you?

Pooja I'm fine, Please be careful; I've heard that the Corona Virus is wreaking on the inhabitants of Chennai.

Yes, Kalpana, Don't worry, I'm at home and obeying all safety protocols.

Meanwhile, kalpana told the plans and their shortcomings, ranted her heart out."

Kalpana was furious by Kapil's attitude and decided to phone his younger brother, even though she already had all of Kapil's contact information but had never attempted to contact anybody from his family, as they both wanted to meet first before revealing to their families. She dialled Rahul Sharma's number.

"Hello! Who is this? Rahul enquired.

I wanted to connect with Kapil, but he is not answering my phone, and I am an old acquaintance of his, Kalpana answered.

Okay! Kapil is in the hospital, infected with a virus, so the doctor isolated him and told him to keep away from mobile radiation, Rahul replied with sorrowful voice."

She hung up the phone. Her eyes were numb, she was terrified, and her spine began shivering. She hadn't ever given this a thought

She shut herself in her room and sobbed uncontrollably; she was terrified; she didn't want to lose Kapil at any cost; and, moreover, since her father's death, she had become hypersensitive to the pain of losing people.

She sobbed a lot that night as she grieved.

"Kalpana!!, The door knocks.

Please come out and have your dinner.

Kalpana was unable to pronounce a single syllable due to such a choked throat. Se responded with great courage.

No, Amma, I'm going to fall asleep."

Kalyani knocked on the door once more, and entered as the door opened

"She inquired, "What append?" with a peculiar voice

Is everything okay with you? You seem to break down and cry, don't you?

Amma, my stoamch is acing, so please leave me alone, she responded."

Her mother walked out of the room, looking at the calendar on the wall.

That night, Kalpana witnessed several victim's tragic stories; many families had lost loved ones as a victim of the virus outbreak; Kalpana became deeply frustrated, disappointed, and furious. She attempted to contact Pooja for consolation, but she was unable to reach her.

She poured forth all of her patience, And, with a yell and an angry tone in her voice, She exclaimed

"I WISH I COULD PULL YOU OUT OF THIS PHONE SCREEN TONIGHT AND BE WITH YOU, KAPIL; I DON'T WANT TO LOSE YOU.

MAHADEV, GOD. I WANT TO HUG HIM, I WANT TO BE WITH HIM, I CANNOT LET HIM DIE LIKE THIS, SO PLEASE LET ME SEE MY KAPIL FOR ONCE."

She immediately fainted .

IV

The Healing Flash

Kalpana awoke to find herself lying on the floor. Her thoughts were still whirling around in her brain. Her body felt heavy, and she kept checking the time. The time was 5:00 a.m. She was starving. So she ate her forgotten meal and went to sleep. She was in bed the next day. It was late afternoon, and she was bereft of energy and unwilling to leave her bed.

In the meantime, Kalyani walked into her room.

"Kalpana? It's late; at the very least, have your food.
Kalpana just agreed with a nod."

Her mind was racing like a lunatic horse because she was so lost. She couldn't seem to break free from Kapil's thoughts.

Regardless, she ate her lunch since she didn't want to tell her mother about her sadness.

She finished her meal and returned to her room. She eventually dozed off.

Then, out of nowhere, a white light flashed from the phone screen. Kalpana awoke because it was so massive and dazzling that she couldn't see around her. The flash of the cellphone screen was too much for her eyes.

She became frightened. She really wanted to leave the room, but she couldn't move an inch. She began chanting "Hanuman chalisa" with her eyes closed firmly.

"Kalpana! A deep, hypnotic voice appeared out of nowhere.

As she slowly opened her eyes, she murmured, "Kapil."

Yes, Kapil was there in front of her, completely nude and emitting white rays of light all around him. He took the towel from the door's hook and wrapped it over his lower body.

Kalpana was startled, her spine chilled as she stared at Kapil. Without blinking, Kapil moved closer to her, so near that she could feel his breath on her face. He held her firmly, her arms around her waist. He grasped her waist and drew her in for a kiss.

They had a kiss!! Kalpana was befuddled and wanted to know what all was going on around her, but she couldn't stop herself from kissing him.

Slowly moving forward, he kissed her on the forehead and wishpered

"Kalpana, I am here. Just relax."

His hypnotic voice made her fall asleep.

V

Her Enigmatic Lover

Her morning alarm went off. She awoke with her eyes wide open, alone on the bed. She was taken aback. She couldn't escape the facts of the night and Kapil's healing kiss.

She began to check her phone, but it appeared to be in tip-top shape. She was puzzled. She couldn't tell if it was a dream or not since it was so vivid that she could still feel the warmth and tenderness of his touch on her lips.

Her thoughts were entirely about the scenario. Later that evening, she wanted to sleep again simply to continue what she had started, so she ate a lot of food at 6:00 PM and went back to sleep. She awoke around 10:00 p.m., feeling her stomach and chest burn like an engine owing to acidity. She made such a blunder that she ended up with acidity.

She realised then that her love would never blossom, and that the only thing she could share with him was the dream.

She became disheartened again and attempted to call Kapil, but the VNR responded.

"The phone number you're trying to call is incorrect."

She was stunned and despondent, so she took a drink of ENO and went back to her bed to attempt to sleep once again.

Something scary passed by once more. She took a step back. The door slammed, and the mobile's light flashed in an instant. The entire room brightened, and Kapil emerged from the phone screen once again.

VI

The Unfortunate Wish

She couldn't believe her eyes. She realised it wasn't a dream anymore. She just wrapped her arm around Kapil and kissed his lips.

Kalpana held his hand in hers and signalled for him to join her. Kapil began kissing her and making sexual moves on her. She first tried to stop him, but she couldn't and soon joined him.

They both fell asleep that night after being intimidated.

Kalpana awoke the next morning to find herself naked on the bed with the door wide open. She sprang out of bed and shut the door behind her.

She put on her clothes. She couldn't understand how any of this could have happened, and where had he gone by morning? During the day, she checked her phone, but nothing had occurred.

She decided to turn off her cellphone tonight. She felt both afraid and overjoyed at the prospect of collapsing into his arms. She was checking her phone and the clock that night with bated breath. She was curious as to what was going on.

Then, at 11:11, the cellphone screen flashed again, and Kapil barely popped his head out. She was taken aback when she saw him again, and she realised that something truly extraordinary was going on with her.

When Kapil emerged, she exhibited little enthusiasm for him, despite the fact that she wished to speak with him. Kapil approached her and attempted to touch her.

""NO!" said Kalpana, sternly. Keep your distance."

"Who are you? She enquired.

"Kalpana, what happened?" Kapil replied. It's me, your love.

"How did you come off this mobile screen?" Kalpana countered. How is this even possible, and why couldn't anybody hear you? Or will they be able to see the enormous flash you set off?"

"Kapil's response was, "I'm not sure. I was in the hospital the last time I checked in. " The doctor advised that I be in quarantine for a few weeks. I wanted to notify you, but I developed an extreme respiratory problem and had to be admitted right away."

"Finally, I came out to meet you over three days, and afterwards, I fell asleep in the mornings, and

when I awoke, I was in this room with you."

"Kalpana was flabbergasted after hearing him speak and responded, "**Kapil, you are correct. At 11:11, I believe I mistakenly wished you off the phone screen.** ""

VII
Kalpana breaks down

Kalpana was both thrilled and scared, as if her desire had suddenly disappeared and the real Kapil was nowhere to be found; she couldn't even contact his phone number or access any of his social media accounts, as if his whole existence was in question.

Kalpana, on the other hand, simply followed him. She was very devoted to him. She sleeps all day so she can spend the night with him.

She'd lost all sense of direction and connection to actuality, and all she could think about was Kapil.

Kalyani, on the other hand, was ill. Kalyani found it difficult to breathe one night while asleep, and her chest was in terrible discomfort. She made her way to Kalpana's room and attempted to knock on the door.

Kalpana, on the other hand, was befuddled by the otherworldly Kapil and couldn't hear her mother's cries for aid. Neighbors rushed out and supported Kalyani in going to the hospital after hearing her mother hammering on her door; neighbours even hammered on her door, but Kalpana could not hear anything.

She noticed her mother was missing when she awoke late that morning.

"Shakuntala, her next-door neighbor, barged in and yelled at her."

"Are you kumbkarani or anything, Kalpana? Your mother had a nervous breakdown just before today. We admitted her to the hospital.

You slept like a corpse. How could you have been so irresponsible?"

Kalpana was caught off guard when she heard this and raced to the hospital, where she found that her mother had also been afflicted with the coronavirus and had been put in the hospital on a ventilator. She stayed in the hospital for the entire night, disoriented and confused as to how she could be so unaware of the current world.

Meanwhile, the doctor approached her and requested that she enter the cabin.

""Come on, Kalpana," the doctor murmured.

"Doctor, is everything all right?" Kalpana inquired, her voice trembling.

"Is there anyone else in your house?" the doctor said after a little pause.

"No doctor?" Kalpana responded. It's just my mother and me. We were both used to being alone.

"Dear, I'm sorry your mother has died," the doctor said quietly as he rose up and moved closer

to Kalpana. "We might be able to save her."

"Kalpana's spine tingled and she was taken aback. "We have many patients like your mother," the doctor said. "Be brave." We can't give her over to you for any death traditions or rituals since her corpse is infected with the virus."

The doctor went right away since there were so many patients. A nurse stood behind them, comforting Kalpana.

Kalpana was completely lost, as if her eyes had stopped sobbing, and she couldn't believe what had transpired in such a short period of time.

She did, however, return to her residence.

Shakuntala Aunty had been expecting her. Aunty wept aloud as she held Kalpana. Kalpana was still stunned and unable to react. Her eyes were numb, and she fell unconscious.

VIII

Struggle of Kalpana

When she recovered consciousness, she was greeted by Shakuntala Aunty and Pooja. Pooja was filled with emotion and snatched Kalpana in her arms, unwilling to let go.

> *"Kalpana," Pooja said, her voice cracking. Is everything okay with you? How could all of this take place in such a short period of time?"*

She was bereft of all hope. She hadn't said anything at the time. She burst out louder as she peered into Pooja's eyes. She screamed and yelled like a lunatic. Her grief had just reached the house's roof. All the neighbours hurried over to Pooja's house because she was so noisy. Everyone came up to her and comforted her. None of them, however, were successful.

Pooja came to sit with Kalpana later that evening and brought her a glass of raw milk. Kalpana continued to refuse a sip, and she simply ranted to Pooja about all that had happened to her in the previous months.

Pooja was taken aback and became terrified, so she embraced Kalpana and murmured, "Relax!!!"

When Pooja was around, Kalpana's problems always seemed to have a solution.Kalpana moved next door to Pooja's house when her father died. The two became friends and shared everything about their lives' ups and downs.

Later that night, Poopja was preoccupied with what Kalpana had said, and she was determined to help Kalpana overcome her mysterious problems. Pooja and her family are highly devout, and the guru used to assist them through all of their life troubles. Pooja's father is an architect, and he always seeks Guruji's advice before beginning any new construction building projects.

So the next day, Pooja went to meet Guruji Krishnadev by herself. Unlike the other brahmans, he was extremely practical and used to impart a lot of spiritual information. Pooja met and told her everything Kalpana had informed her of.

""I could understand that her grief for that boy made her wish this," Guru ji said. Perhaps her desire came true, but if she can manage her emotions, she will be capable of overcoming all that has happened to her."

Gurji was well aware that her long-lost mother would never return, but he did not want Kalpana to return to that mysterious person in order to alleviate her mother's grief.

So he requested Pooja to return to her home, while Guruji and his shishya arrived the next day to meet Kalpana.

IX

The Right prayer

Guruji noticed Kalpana, who was seated opposite the window, distraught. He approached her.

"Kalpana Beta, Guruji called her."

Kalpana got to her feet and stood up. He promptly blessed her and instructed her to prepare for some rites.

Kalpana was taken aback and glanced at Pooja with a puzzled expression. Pooja approached and took Kalpana with her. She dressed her in saffron linen and delivered her to Guru Ji.

Guruji want to awaken the true Kalpana and assist her in overcoming her irrational attachments and sufferings.

"Come sit on the floor and take three deep breaths while shutting your eyes. Guruji instructed"

Kalpana did the same thing.

"Kalpana, I'm going to ask you some questions. If you see it's appropriate, respond to them. Guruji Claims

First and foremost, Kalpana, what is your greatest fear?"

"I don't want to lose anybody, Kalpana stated."

""Who do you not want to lose, Kalpana?" Guruji responded."

"Kalpana paused for a long time, tears rolling down her cheeks. She said, "I have lost all those whom I dreaded losing.""

"Guruji said,

Okay, take a deep breath... Was it fate or your fault, Kalpana, that you lost all of them?"

"With her eyes wide open, Kalpana gasped! Was it my fault?!?"

"Consider the situation. Your father passed away. That was destiny. But how did you manage to lose both your mother and Kapil? Guruji enquired."

"Kalpana became outraged and said, "I hadn't harmed anybody in any way." I learned that Kapil had been admitted to the hospital. I had a nervous breakdown. Then he returned to me, because of which I had to say goodbye to my mother. I was really taken with him. " What makes you think it's *my fault?"*

"Is it love or a crazy obsession? Guruji questioned"

""If it had been simply pure love, you would have wished him good health, you would have wished him life, but instead you ended up wishing him out of the phone screen!" he said. As a result, every night he happened to come out exclusively for you, he became supernatural."

"..Is this what you call love?
You're trying to get away from him, Kalpana, but keep in mind what you did to him."

Kalpana was lost and speechless after listening to Guruji. She couldn't respond since she didn't have anything to say. At that time, she acknowledged her blunder and proceeded to apologise to Guru Ji, bowing in front of him.

"He offered her comfort. "relax" he added."

"Get up, Kalpana, and return to your previous spot. Guru Ji instructed"

"Listen, Kalpana, every human on the planet makes selfish wishes, and if God fulfilled all of them, everyone on the planet, like you, would suffer, which is why our wishes rarely come true and god waits to teach us the true meaning of prayer."

Kalpana acknowledged his thoughts with a nod. After that, Guruji encouraged her to meditate and assisted her in stimulating her root chakra.

The root chakra is responsible for controlling and balancing emotions.

As the week goes by, Kalpana meditates and attempts to unlock the whole of her 7 chakras.

X

The Wake Up

Kalpana was lien and had finished healing her crown chakras; she was engaged in meditation and desired to liberate all of her attachments.

The white light suddenly sprang out of her brain, causing excruciating pain. At a moment when Kalpana couldn't take it any longer, she abruptly opened her eyes wide open.

Huh!!!, Kalpana wakes up and discover she's in bed as she hears a loud voice

> *"say, "Doctor!!! Doctor!!!," Medical team and a nurse came up to her."*

She only looked at a woman and recognized it was her mother, Kalyani, and then she lost out once again.

She awoke after an hour when her mother approached her room. She was astonished and just glared at her mother without winking.

She couldn't even utter a syllable as she was too feeble. Her feet and hands were just so vulnerable as well. Her mother came close to her

*"She stated. Kalpana, beta!!!
Kalpana, beta!!! She kissed her forehead and said,
"You are alive, and I am really so glad to have you
back."*

Kalpana was so dazed and exhausted that she couldn't think of anything.

The day went by. Kalpana was able to get up after a week and inquired in hushed tones.

*"Mom, I'm not sure what's going on with me.
Kalyani said, "You were in comma for the past
five years,"*

*"when you found out about Kapil, you collapsed,
and the doctor stated us that you had merely gone
into comma."*

*"Kalpana then recollect the night when she was
sobbing uncontrollably that she collapsed and
smacked her head on the wall.
Meanwhile, she inquired about Kapil, leading
her mother to hesitate and took long pause.....*

WHAT HAPPEND TO KAPIL?

IS HE ALIVE ?

WILL THEY MEET AGAIN?

To be continued in my next book , Enigmatic Lover - The Conclusion II

www.ingramcontent.com/pod-product-compliance
Lightning Source LLC
Chambersburg PA
CBHW031006180726
47993CB00018B/1589